Muppet TREASURE ISLAND ™

Starring Jim Henson's Muppets™

Adapted (loosely) by Ellen Weiss
from the movie *Muppet Treasure Island*

Original screenplay by Jerry Juhl & Kirk R. Thatcher and James V. Hart
Based (very, very loosely) on the novel by Robert Louis Stevenson

Illustrated by Tom Brannon

 A MUPPET PRESS / GOLDEN BOOK

Jim Hawkins was a poor orphan boy and his life was hard. He worked long hours at the Admiral Benbow Inn, waiting on rowdy sailors.

His only friends in the world were a rat named Rizzo and a—well, a something-or-other called Gonzo.

One of the guests at the inn was an old pirate named Billy Bones. Billy loved to tell Jim about a treasure that was buried on a far-off island. Billy hinted that he had a map to the treasure.

"But watch out," said Billy. "Beware the one-legged man!"

One night the inn was stormed by a band of
blackhearted pirates looking for Billy's treasure map.
"Take it," Billy told Jim. "Run!"
Jim and his friends escaped with the map.

The three friends went to see young Squire Trelawney, who agreed to help them find Treasure Island. He found jobs for them as cabin boys on the good ship *Hispaniola*.

They were off to search for the treasure!

The captain of the ship was named Smollett. Although he was said to have a bad temper, he actually seemed rather nice.

But the crew was a nasty bunch of cutthroats, villains, and scoundrels.

The ship's cook was a man with one leg named
Long John Silver. Jim remembered Billy Bones's
warning about this man. But Long John seemed
so friendly.

He couldn't be the bad guy—could he?

The pirates suspected that Jim had the treasure map.
So one night they searched his things. But they couldn't
find the map. Jim had it in a bag around his neck.

Captain Smollett found out that the pirates had broken into Jim's cabin. "You must let me keep the treasure map for you," he told Jim. So Jim let Smollett lock it up in a strongbox.

Because he thought Long John Silver was his friend, Jim told him where the map was hidden.

But Long John had only pretended to be Jim's friend. He and his evil pals broke into Captain Smollett's box and stole the map. The next day Jim found his friends in the ship's galley. They were inside a barrel, eating apples.

Suddenly Long John and the others came into the galley, laughing and joking about the treasure map they had stolen.

Jim was shocked! So Long John Silver *was* the evil pirate Bones had warned about! But there was no time to do anything because suddenly they heard the cry from above: "*Land ho!*"

Long John invited Jim to go ashore with him.

Jim was frightened. "I can't," he said.

So Long John tricked him. He asked Jim to hand him his crutch and then pulled the boy into the boat with him.

Captain Smollett wasn't worried about the stolen map. "We'll leave Silver and his men here and return in a year with an honest crew," he declared. But then Rizzo pointed out the window. "We can't leave," he said. "The pirates have Jim!"

There was nothing for Smollett to do but go ashore and rescue Jim. The pirates were already on the trail of the treasure.

But when Captain Smollett reached the island, he was in for a nasty surprise. It was ruled by a ferocious tribe of wild boars!

The King of the Boars ordered his gang to tie up Smollett, Gonzo, and Rizzo. The boars sang and danced while they waited for their Queen, Boom Sha-Kal-A-Kal, to arrive.

"Smolly? Can it be you?" gasped the Queen of the Boars.

It turned out that the Queen was really Benjamina Gunn. Once, she had almost married Smollett, but he'd left her at the altar. So she'd gone off with a pirate captain and ended up on this island.

Benjamina was still pretty mad at Captain Smollett.

Soon Long John Silver captured Smollett and
Benjamina, demanding to know where the treasure
was hidden. Benjamina said it was at her house and
the pirates ran off to find it.

Since they were hanging around together,
Benjamina decided to forgive her old sweetheart.

While Silver searched for the treasure, Jim and his friends escaped back to the ship and sailed it to shore to rescue Smollett and Benjamina.

After a big fight the captain and his lady were saved!

By this time Silver had returned to the ship with the trunks of treasure. When things began looking bad for the pirates, he decided to slip away in one of the small boats.

Unfortunately, the boat leaked. There was nothing Silver could do but swim ashore and spend a nice long time with the boars.

At last it was time for the *Hispaniola* to set sail for home. The adventure of Treasure Island was over—but there would be others to come.